Johanna Spyri's

HEIDI

Adapted and abridged by Alice Thorne

Illustrated by Miriam Troop

GROSSET & DUNLAP · PUBLISHERS · NEW YORK

Up the Mountain

FROM THE pleasant old town of Mayenfeld, a shady path leads to the base of the mountains which gaze down upon the little valley. Then the path turns sharply upward, while the keen scent of mountain herbs begins to steal up from the earth.

On a sunny morning in June, a young Swiss woman was climbing the path, leading a little girl by the hand. In spite of the June sun, the child was wearing two dresses, one on top of the other, and a thick red shawl. Thus clad, and wearing heavy shoes, the odd little figure trudged sturdily up the mountain path.

After an hour's climbing, they reached a tiny village midway between the valley and the Alm. But the young woman did not pause until a voice from the doorway of one of the cottages called, "Wait a moment, Dete! If you're going farther, I'll come along with you."

At this Dete stopped. Immediately the little girl seated herself on the ground.

"Are you tired, Heidi?" Dete asked.

"No, I'm hot," the child replied.

"Never mind," said Dete. "We'll be there in an hour."

At this moment, the woman who had called to Dete came up. "Where are you going with the child, Dete?" she asked. "She's your sister's little girl—the orphan—isn't she?"

"Yes, Barbel," Dete replied. "I'm taking her up to the Alm Uncle. She's going to live with him."

"What!" exclaimed Barbel. "Live with the Alm Uncle! Impossible, Dete! The old man will send you back a good deal faster than you came, that's certain."

"Oh, no, he won't," returned Dete. "After all, he's her grandfather, and he must do something for her. I've cared for Heidi ever since her parents died. But I can't give up the chance of a good position in Frankfort for the sake of a child. Let *him* take care of her now!"

"That's all very well—if he were like other folk," said Barbel. "But I wouldn't be in that child's shoes for anything! Why, that old man up there hasn't a word to say to a living soul! When he comes down here—once a year, maybe—with those bushy eyebrows and that tangled beard, everybody gets out of his way in a hurry!"

"All the same, he *is* her grandfather," Dete insisted.

"Come—tell me," Barbel coaxed. "Is the old man such a terror as they say?"

"Whether he always was, I don't know," Dete answered. "After all, I'm only twenty-six, and he'll never see seventy again. But I don't deny I *could* tell you a thing or two about him."

Dete glanced around for Heidi, but could not see her.

"There she is," Barbel said, pointing. "Up the mountain with Peter the goatherd and his goats. He'll take care of the child for you."

"He won't have to take much care of her," remarked Dete. "She's not foolish for her five years, and a good thing, too—she'll need her wits, for the old man hasn't anything in the world but his two goats and his cottage."

"But there was a time when he was a great deal better off, eh?" Barbel said.

"I should say he was!" exclaimed Dete. "Why, his father left him the finest farm in Domleschg. But he did not take care of his land and his money. When he had nothing left in the world, he disappeared. Then, after fifteen years, he came back to Dorfli, and here he lived with his boy, Tobias. Tobias was a good lad, and everybody liked him. But the old man was suspicious and unfriendly. We always called him Uncle, because we are related to him. Then, after he went to live all alone on the Alm, everybody took to calling him the Alm Uncle."

"But what happened to Tobias?" Barbel asked.

"Tobias married my sister, Adelheid," Dete said. "But the poor fellow was killed in an accident only two years later. Adelheid fell ill of grief, and just a few weeks after he was killed, she died too.

"Then people began to say that the sad thing that had happened was a judgment on the old man for his sinful life. This made him fierce and surly, and at last he went up the Alm, where he has lived ever since. Mother and I took Adelheid's baby. But now that Mother is gone, and I have the chance of this good position, I'm going to take it!"

"And leave the child with the Alm Uncle?" exclaimed Barbel. "How can you have the heart, Dete?"

"What do you mean?" demanded Dete sharply. "I've done my duty by her." Then she asked abruptly, "How far are you going, Barbel? We're halfway up the Alm."

"I stop here. I want to speak to Peter's mother, who does my spinning for me in the winter," Barbel told her. "Well, good-by, Dete."

Dete shook hands with her friend and watched her walk toward a tiny, weather-beaten cottage a little distance off. This was the home of Peter the goatherd, a boy about eleven years old. Every morning Peter went down to Dorfli to fetch the goats. He would drive them far up the mountain where they could munch the short grass and herbs until sundown. When dusk began to fall, Peter would bring his light-footed little herd back down to the village.

He lived with his mother and his blind grandmother—his father was dead—but he saw very little of them. Every morning he had to be off at daybreak. And at night he had barely time enough to eat some bread and drink some milk before he crept into bed and fell fast asleep.

Since the children were nowhere in sight, Dete climbed higher and looked about impatiently. Meanwhile, Peter and Heidi had turned off upon another path. Heidi, hindered by all her clothes, was panting with weariness. She made no complaint, but looked wistfully at Peter, who, with his bare feet and scanty clothes, skipped nimbly along.

Suddenly Heidi seated herself on the ground. In a twinkling, she had pulled off her shoes, her stockings, and the thick shawl. Next, she slipped out of her dress and unhooked the one that was under it. In a moment she was standing there dressed only in her little shirt and her light petticoat. She stretched her arms delightedly in the air. Then she placed her clothes in a neat heap, and ran after Peter and the goats.

When Peter saw what she had done, he grinned widely but said nothing. Feeling much better now, Heidi followed him to the summit of the hill, where Dete was now waiting.

Dete took one look at the little girl and cried, "Heidi! What have you done with your dresses and your shawl and your shoes?"

The child pointed down the mountain and replied, "There!"

"Heidi, you bad girl!" Dete exclaimed. "Whatever made you do such a thing?"

"I didn't need them," Heidi said simply.

"You—what!" shrieked Dete. "Here—Peter! Don't just stand there. Run down quickly and get those clothes!"

Peter was off down the slope like a flash. He was back up again so swiftly that Dete had to praise him for his speed. She gave him a coin, and Peter beamed with delight. Three-quarters of an hour later they reached the Alm. There, on an overhanging ledge of the mountain, stood the hut of the Alm Uncle. It was exposed to the winds, but was bathed in the sunlight, too, and had a view over the whole valley.

Behind the hut stood three great pine trees. Farther back, the mountain heights lifted themselves toward the sky.

The Alm Uncle had built himself a bench against the side of the hut which overlooked the valley. Here, with his pipe in his mouth, the old man himself sat quietly watching the three who were approaching.

Heidi was the first to reach the top. She went at once to the old man, laid her little hand in his, and said, "Good day, Grandfather."

"Eh? What's this?" said the old man roughly. But after a moment, he shook hands with the child. His keen eyes beneath his dense gray eyebrows regarded her sharply. Heidi returned the sharp gaze steadily.

Dete now boldly approached the Alm Uncle.

"Good day, Uncle," she said briskly. "I've brought you your grandchild. I don't suppose you recognize Heidi—you haven't seen her since she was a year old."

"So?" returned the old man slowly. "Well, what does she want of me?" Then, without warning, he turned sharply on Peter. "Be off with you—you and your goats. And see that you take mine along too."

The frightened Peter disappeared without a word.

"The child must stay with you," Dete said to the old man. "I've done my duty by her for four years. Now you can do yours."

"Humph!" growled the Alm Uncle. His eyes flashed dangerously. "Well—and if she starts to whine and whimper for you—such young children do—what must I do then?"

"That's your affair," returned Dete with a shrug. "But if harm comes to her, *you* will answer for it! Good-by, Heidi!" she added quickly, and fled down the mountain.

WHEN DETE had gone, the old man returned to his bench. He sat there in silence, blowing out clouds of smoke from his pipe.

Heidi, meanwhile, cheerfully began looking over her new home. First, she discovered the stall for the goats. Finding it empty, she went around to the back of the hut. The wind was sighing through the branches of the pine trees, and the child stood beneath them, listening until the sound died away. Then she wandered back to where her grandfather was sitting. After a moment, she went up to him, laid her hand on his shoulder, and regarded him in silence. The old man glanced up. "What now?" he demanded.

"I want to see the inside of the hut, Grandfather," Heidi said.

"Come along, then." He rose to lead the way. "And take your bundle."

"I don't need it any more," Heidi said calmly.

"Why don't you need it?" the old man asked.

"I'd rather be like the goats. They don't have a lot of clothes to bother them," replied Heidi simply.

"Well — well — as you please. But bring your things along anyway. We'll put them away in the closet."

Heidi obeyed him. Then he opened the door of the hut. She saw a fairly large room, with a table and chair in the middle. A sleeping bunk was in one corner, and in another the hearth, with a great kettle hanging over it. The old man pulled open a closet door, and Heidi tucked her bundle in as far back as possible. Then she looked about the room.

"Where shall I sleep, Grandfather?" she asked.

"Where you please."

Heidi began to poke into every corner to find a suitable place. Presently she spied a small ladder, leading to a hayloft. She climbed up. Then, from the top of the ladder, she gave a shout of delight. The floor of the loft was strewn with fresh, sweet-smelling hay, and from a little round window, she could look down upon the whole valley.

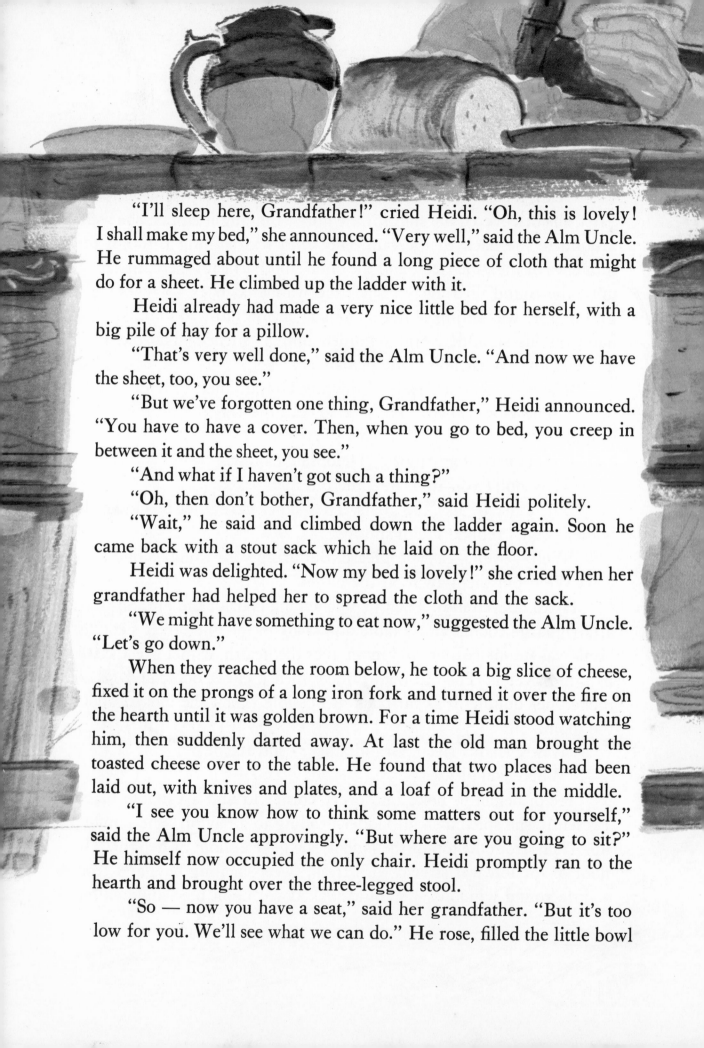

"I'll sleep here, Grandfather!" cried Heidi. "Oh, this is lovely! I shall make my bed," she announced. "Very well," said the Alm Uncle. He rummaged about until he found a long piece of cloth that might do for a sheet. He climbed up the ladder with it.

Heidi already had made a very nice little bed for herself, with a big pile of hay for a pillow.

"That's very well done," said the Alm Uncle. "And now we have the sheet, too, you see."

"But we've forgotten one thing, Grandfather," Heidi announced. "You have to have a cover. Then, when you go to bed, you creep in between it and the sheet, you see."

"And what if I haven't got such a thing?"

"Oh, then don't bother, Grandfather," said Heidi politely.

"Wait," he said and climbed down the ladder again. Soon he came back with a stout sack which he laid on the floor.

Heidi was delighted. "Now my bed is lovely!" she cried when her grandfather had helped her to spread the cloth and the sack.

"We might have something to eat now," suggested the Alm Uncle. "Let's go down."

When they reached the room below, he took a big slice of cheese, fixed it on the prongs of a long iron fork and turned it over the fire on the hearth until it was golden brown. For a time Heidi stood watching him, then suddenly darted away. At last the old man brought the toasted cheese over to the table. He found that two places had been laid out, with knives and plates, and a loaf of bread in the middle.

"I see you know how to think some matters out for yourself," said the Alm Uncle approvingly. "But where are you going to sit?" He himself now occupied the only chair. Heidi promptly ran to the hearth and brought over the three-legged stool.

"So — now you have a seat," said her grandfather. "But it's too low for you. We'll see what we can do." He rose, filled the little bowl

with milk, and set it on his own chair. He drew it up to the stool so that Heidi had a little chair and table all to herself. Then he cut a generous slice of bread and a piece of the cheese and put them before her.

"There you are. Now eat away," he said, and sat down on a corner of the table to eat his own meal. Heidi was very thirsty after her long and dusty journey. Taking a firm hold of her bowl of milk, she drank without stopping until there was not a drop left.

"How does the milk suit you?" asked the Alm Uncle.

"I've never tasted any milk so good," declared Heidi.

"Then you shall have some more." And once again the Alm Uncle filled her bowl. Heidi ate and drank contentedly.

When the meal was over, the Alm Uncle went out to put the goat stall in order. Heidi followed him, watching how he swept it and then strewed it with fresh straw. Then he went off to his workshop and cut some straight sticks. He fashioned a smooth, round board, boring holes in it, into which he fixed the sticks.

"Now, what do you think this is, Heidi?" he asked.

"That's my chair!" cried Heidi. "It's just like yours, only higher."

"She knows how to use her eyes," the Alm Uncle muttered.

Thus the afternoon passed, and evening drew near. The wind now rushed through the pine trees with increasing vigor, its music filling Heidi's ears. All at once, through the dusk, came a shrill whistle. The Alm Uncle went out to meet young Peter, who in the midst of his flock, was leaping toward them down the mountain.

The Alm Uncle held out a little salt in each hand. Soon two slender goats, one white, the other brown, stepped out of the herd and began to lick his fingers eagerly.

"The white one is Little Swan, and the brown one is Little Bear," the Alm Uncle told Heidi.

When Peter had driven off the rest of the herd toward Dorfli, the Alm Uncle sat down and began to milk the white goat.

"Here is your supper now," he said when he had filled a bowl with milk and given Heidi a slice of bread. "Eat it and then run off to bed. I must put the goats into the stall, so good night and sleep well."

"Good night, Grandfather. Good night, Little Swan. Good night, Little Bear," Heidi cried. Then she ate her bread and milk and went to bed. In a little while, curled up in the thick, fragrant hay, she was sleeping as sweetly as if she were lying in a palace.

The Mountain Pasture

THE BRIGHT morning sun awakened Heidi early. For a moment, she sat blinking in bewilderment, and then she recalled the events of the past day. Filled with a joyous sense of freedom, she sprang up and dressed herself quickly. Then she climbed down the ladder, eager to see what this new day on the Alm would bring forth.

Peter was standing at the door of the hut in the midst of his flock.

"How would you like to go up to the pasture with the Goat-General?" asked the Alm Uncle. Heidi's answer was a prance of joy.

A big tub of water was standing at the door, and Heidi ran to it. She washed until her cheeks shone. Meanwhile, the Alm Uncle shouted to Peter, "Here, Goat-General, bring me your haversack!"

Peter obeyed. His round face wore a look of mild wonder, which changed to amazement as the old man thrust into his bag a great slice of cheese, nearly three times as large as Peter's own piece.

"Here is a cup, too," said the Alm Uncle. "At noonday, you must fill the cup with milk for Heidi. She is in your care, remember that."

The two children set off merrily, Heidi leaping on ahead in delight. The wind had swept every cloud from the deep blue summer sky, and the sun warmed the mountain slopes, all carpeted with flowers. Never in her life had Heidi seen or dreamed of such flowers — red primroses, fringed gentians, blue as the sky itself, and golden rockroses with their thorny petals — all beckoning to her.

"Come on," Peter urged. "We have a good way to go yet." And he added slyly, "Way up on the highest cliff a great eagle sits and screeches." Immediately, Heidi ran to him. The goats, too, pressed forward eagerly toward the pasture where, in the middle of the morning, Peter always stopped to rest.

When they reached it, Peter unslung his haversack and dropped it in a little hollow. Then he stretched out on the warm grass and promptly fell asleep. But Heidi, bright-eyed and quiet as a mouse, sat drinking in the peaceful beauty of the scene. A long time passed, while Peter slept and the goats nibbled and munched among the bushes.

Then, all of a sudden, a harsh scream startled the little girl. Overhead, a huge bird was circling through the air and uttering shrill cries.

"Peter! Peter! Wake up!" Heidi cried in terror. "It's the eagle!"

The boy started to his feet, but already the great bird was rising higher and higher into the air. As they both stood gazing upward, it vanished beyond the gray peaks of the mountains.

"Where has he gone?" asked Heidi wonderingly.

"Home . . . to his nest."

"It is way up there? Really? Oh, it must be beautiful to live up in the crags like that!" exclaimed Heidi. "But why does he scream so?"

"Because — why, because he has to," Peter said lamely, and he turned to whistle to his goats. They came, pushing and butting each other with their horns. While Heidi played with them, Peter laid out the noonday meal. He spread the haversack on the grass and put Heidi's generous portions of bread and cheese on one side and his own scanty lunch on the other. Then, following instructions, he took the cup and milked Little Swan until the cup was brimming.

They ate with hearty appetites. But after a few minutes, Heidi broke off a big piece of bread and cheese and held it out to Peter.

"You can eat this too, if you like," she said. "I've had enough."

Peter gaped at her, unable to believe that anybody ever had enough to eat. But with a quick nod of thanks, he fell upon it.

"Peter," said Heidi, "tell me the names of the goats."

Promptly, the boy pointed them out, one by one. The big one who was always butting his comrades with his strong horns was Turk. None of the others dared defy him except the slender, graceful Thistlefinch, who often astonished the bigger goat by his boldness. The little white one was Snowhopper. He bleated so piteously that Heidi ran and put her arms around him.

"He's crying because his mother was taken away yesterday and sold in the market," Peter explained.

"Oh, you poor little Snowhopper!" cried Heidi. "Don't cry any more. If anything makes you sad, you can come right to me."

Snowhopper seemed to understand that his woes had at last aroused some pity, for he snuggled contentedly in Heidi's arms.

"The prettiest of all are Little Swan and Little Bear," Heidi said.

"That's true," Peter admitted. "That's because — Hey!" he broke off with a cry of alarm. Leaping to his feet, he sprang forward. Thistlefinch had strayed close to the edge of the cliff. Peter flung himself on the ground and seized the goat by one leg. The silly little animal set up a shrill bleating. Struggling to free himself from Peter's frantic grasp, he drew them both still nearer to the edge of the cliff.

"Heidi! Heidi!" shouted Peter. But Heidi already had seen the danger. Quickly gathering a handful of sweet-smelling herbs, she held them out to the struggling animal.

"Come, now, don't be silly," she coaxed. "Don't you know that if you fell down on those rocks, you'd break your leg?"

Thistlefinch stopped struggling and followed Heidi, nibbling eagerly at the herbs she held out to him. Gradually, she moved back from the edge of the cliff. But Peter, badly frightened, meant to punish the rebellious goat. When they were safely back to the flock, he raised his stick to beat Thistlefinch.

"No, no, Peter!" Heidi cried, clinging to him with all her strength. "You mustn't beat him! See how frightened he is!"

"He deserves it and he's going to catch it," growled Peter.

"I say you shan't!" cried Heidi. "I won't let you!"

Peter stared at her in amazement. He had never seen her angry before. He let his stick fall. It occurred to him he might make a bargain.

"Well," he said, "I'll let him alone if you'll give me some of your bread and cheese again tomorrow."

"You can have all of it!" Heidi cried. "But you must never, never beat the goats again. Do you hear?"

"It's all one to me," Peter said with a shrug. And he released Thistlefinch, who bounded away joyfully.

The day drew gradually to an end, and the sun was beginning to sink beyond the western rim of snow-capped mountain peaks. Heidi sat on the grass, watching the golden light that slid over the green slopes. Then, all at once, on the distant pinnacles, there broke forth a splendor so sublime that the child cried out in awe.

"Peter! The mountains are on fire! Look, Peter! There is fire over the eagle's nest, and on the rocks and fir trees!"

"It's always like that," Peter said calmly. "That isn't really fire."

"What is it, then?" cried Heidi.

"I don't know. It just gets that way by itself," said Peter.

Slowly, the splendor faded, and the calm, gray shades of twilight began to steal over the mountain peaks.

"It'll be just like that again tomorrow," Peter said. "Come on. It's time to go home."

Heidi's thoughts were so occupied with the events of the day that she did not utter a word until they reached the hut.

"Well," said the Alm Uncle when Peter had departed with his flock, "how did it go with you?"

Heidi's black eyes sparkled. "Oh, Grandfather! It was so beautiful! You should have seen the sky — all rosy, and the snow on the mountains so red that they looked as if they were on fire!"

The Alm Uncle smiled and bade her go and wash, while he milked the goats and prepared their supper.

A little later, Heidi, fresh and clean, was perched up on her stool beside her grandfather with a brimming cup of milk before her.

"Grandfather," she asked, "why does the eagle scream so?"

The old man's face changed, and he did not reply immediately. Then, with a strange gleam in his eyes, he said:

"He is jeering at the people who pass their miserable lives in the crowded towns and villages below — huddled together like sheep, and making one another wretched!" As he spoke, his voice rose until it seemed to take on the harsh note of the eagle's cry. "And he says to them, 'If any one of you dared to come away from the herd and make your way alone to the heights, as I do, I would not despise him!'"

Heidi was startled and almost frightened by his unexpected outcry. For a time both of them were silent. But presently Heidi asked again:

"Where did all the fire come from, Grandfather?"

"Well," said the Alm Uncle, gently now, "it's like this. When the sun says good night to the mountains, he throws over them his most beautiful colors so they will not forget him when he comes back to them in the morning."

Heidi was delighted with this explanation. And now that bedtime had come, she climbed up happily to her loft, where she was soon sleeping soundly in the soft and fragrant hay.

DAY AFTER day Heidi and Peter went up to the pasture with the goats. As the summer passed, Heidi grew as brown as a berry. Then autumn came, and there were mornings when the wind blew so hard that the Alm Uncle would not let her go with Peter. "These winds could carry a little one like you into the valley at one puff!" he said.

Then, suddenly, one night the snow fell. In the morning a dazzling white blanket covered the Alm. Winter had come, and after that Peter no longer herded the goats. The snow fell more and more thickly until it was so deep that it reached up to the windows of the hut.

One day there came a loud thumping on the door. A moment later it was pushed open, and there stood Peter. From head to foot he was covered with snow, for he had made his way through high drifts.

"Good afternoon," he said. Then, seating himself as close to the fire as possible, he looked at Heidi, beaming.

"Well, how goes the world with you, Goat-General?" asked the Alm Uncle. "Your army has gone into winter quarters, and you are left to gnaw the pencil, eh?"

"Why does he have to gnaw pencils, Grandfather?" inquired Heidi in surprise.

"Because, in winter, he has to go to school — but it helps to chew up a few pencils while you struggle, eh, Peter?"

"Yes, it does help," said Peter seriously.

Instantly, Heidi had a hundred questions to ask him about school. They chattered away merrily, while the fire dried Peter's dripping clothes, and the short winter afternoon wore away.

By the time supper was over, night had fallen. Peter rose to go. At the door he stopped and announced, "Granny says to please come and see her, Heidi." With this, he left.

The idea of going to visit someone was exciting to Heidi, but the snow was too deep for her to go out. At last, however, the sun shone once more. When Heidi asked her grandfather to take her to the grandmother's cottage, he told her to bundle up.

Outside the hut, Heidi stopped short in delight. The fir trees stood motionless, every bough weighted down with sparkling snow.

The Alm Uncle brought his sled. He tucked her up warmly on it, seated himself behind her, and held her close with his left arm. A moment later, they were sliding down the mountainside through the snow so swiftly that they seemed to be flying. In almost no time at all they had reached the goatherd's cottage.

"Here we are," said the Alm Uncle, as he set Heidi down on the ground. "Run inside, but remember, as soon as it begins to grow dark, you must start for home."

He turned about, dragging his sled behind him, and made his way back up the mountain.

The grandmother's cottage was tiny. Sitting at a table, a woman was sewing, and in the corner, a little old lady was spinning flax.

Heidi walked over to the spinning wheel. Looking at the old lady, she said clearly, "Good day, Granny — here I am."

The old woman raised her head and groped for Heidi's hand.

"Is it really Heidi?" she asked. "The child who now lives with the Alm Uncle?"

"Yes, I am Heidi. My grandfather brought me to see you. We came down the mountain on the sled."

"On the *sled*?" repeated Granny in her quavering voice. "And yet the little hand is so warm! Tell me, Brigida, what does she look like?"

Peter's mother had risen from her chair and was looking intently at Heidi. "She is slender and small like her mother," Brigida answered. "And she has black eyes and curly hair like her father — and like the Alm Uncle, too, when he was young. She resembles them both."

"Look, Granny," Heidi exclaimed, pointing to the window. "That shutter is loose. My grandfather could fix it with a nail so it wouldn't swing back and forth like that."

"I cannot see it, dear child, but I can hear it very well. When the wind blows hard at night, I hear the whole house groaning, so that I am in terror lest it fall down and kill us all."

"But why can't you see how the shutter swings, Granny?" asked Heidi, puzzled.

"I cannot see anything," answered the old woman. "I am blind."

Heidi covered her face with her hands and burst into tears. "Oh, Granny, Granny!" she sobbed. "Can't *anyone* make you see?"

Heidi very seldom cried, but she felt sorrow as deeply as she felt joy, and Granny could not comfort her for a long time.

"Listen, child, I will tell you something," she said, taking Heidi's hand in hers. "When one cannot see, one hears all the more gladly a kindly word, and yours have made me very happy. Come, now, sit here beside me and tell me what you do up there on the Alm."

Heidi dried her tears. "Just wait, Granny," she said, her face brightening. "I will tell Grandfather everything. *He* can make you see, and he'll fix the cottage so it won't ever rattle and shake any more."

Cheered by this plan, in which she had perfect confidence, she began to chatter away, telling the old woman about life on the Alm.

Their talk was interrupted by a banging of the door, and in came Peter. Seeing Heidi, he stopped short, grinning widely.

"Good evening, Peter," said Heidi gaily.

"What!" exclaimed Granny. "Is it already time for the boy to be back from school? It has been many a year since the day has passed so quickly. Good evening, Peterkin. How did the reading go today?"

"Just the same."

The old woman sighed. "Dear, dear, I thought there might be a change."

"What kind of change, Granny?" asked Heidi.

"I hoped that he might be able to read by now," said the grandmother wistfully. "You see, I have a book — full of lovely hymns I haven't heard for many years. I had hoped Peter might learn to read them to me."

Peter's mother now rose to light the lamp, and Heidi sprang up.

"I must go, Granny," she said. "I promised Grandfather I would come home as soon as it got dark."

Just as she came out of the cottage, she saw the Alm Uncle striding down the mountainside.

"Well, I see that you keep your word, Heidi," he said.

As soon as Heidi and her grandfather reached the hut, Heidi began breathlessly, "Grandfather, tomorrow we must take the hammer and nails and fix Granny's cottage so that it doesn't creak and rattle any more!"

"Eh? Must? We *must*?" repeated the Alm Uncle, drawing his fierce eyebrows together. "Who told you that?"

"Nobody told me," said Heidi. "But you see, the cottage is old and shaky, and when the wind blows it makes such noises that Granny gets frightened and can't sleep. No one can help her but you, so we'll go tomorrow, won't we, Grandfather?"

For a few moments the Alm Uncle said nothing, but looked steadily into Heidi's black eyes that shone with unquestioning confidence in him. Then he said briefly, "Yes, we will go tomorrow."

He kept his promise. Early the following morning, the sled was flying down to the cottage where, as on the day before, the Alm Uncle bade Heidi go in and remember to leave as soon as darkness fell. Then he himself went around to the back of the little house.

Heidi had barely unlatched the door, when the blind woman cried joyfully, "It's the child!"

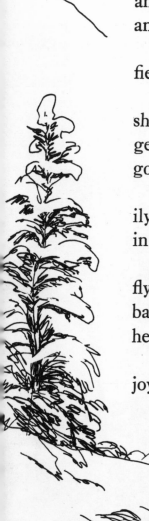

Heidi ran to her and, drawing a little stool close to her side, began to tell the old lady a thousand new things. But in the midst of her lively chatter, the whole cottage suddenly trembled under the force of repeated blows.

"Dear Heaven!" shrieked Granny, starting up and shaking with terror. "Now it is really falling upon us!"

"No, no, Granny!" Heidi hastily reassured her. "Don't be frightened — Grandfather is just hammering in nails to make the walls safe!"

The poor old woman could hardly believe her ears.

"Did you hear that, Brigida?" she asked in a quavering voice. "Can it be possible?"

The Alm Uncle nailed up loosened boards, mended the gaps in walls and roof, and fastened the broken, creaking shutters. By the time he had finished, it was nightfall. Heidi ran out to him just as he was bringing his sled around to the door.

Thus the winter passed, bringing into the life of the blind old grandmother a new joy. Her days were no longer dark and melancholy, for even when Heidi was not with her, she had the delight of looking forward to her visits.

And so well had the Alm Uncle done his work that even when the fiercest winds blew down the mountain, the walls and shutters no longer groaned and shook. Instead of lying awake all night in terror, Granny could sleep as she had not slept in years.

 *Visitors on the Alm*

TWO WINTERS had passed, and Heidi was nearly eight years old. Her grandfather had taught her many things, and she was as good a little goatherd as Peter himself.

One sunny March morning, Heidi was startled by the unexpected appearance of an elderly man dressed in black.

"I think you must be Heidi," he said to her. "Will you tell me where I can find your grandfather?"

"He is in the hut," Heidi said, "making wooden spoons." She led the stranger indoors where the Alm Uncle was sitting at the table. At the visitor's greeting, he raised his head, and a gleam came into his dark eyes. Rising from his stool, he said quietly, "Good day, Pastor."

"It has been a long time since I have seen you, neighbor," said the pastor, seating himself on the wooden stool the Alm Uncle had drawn up for him. "I have come today," he continued, with a glance at Heidi, "to talk about a certain matter with you."

"Heidi," said the Alm Uncle, "go and play with the goats."

"The child should have been sent to school a year ago," said the pastor, when Heidi had gone. "And certainly you should let her attend the school in Dorfli this winter."

"It is my intention *not* to send her to school," the Alm Uncle said grimly. "She grows and thrives with the goats — with the birds and all good things, and she learns no evil from them!"

"It may be true that she learns no evil, but she learns nothing else either. Do you really believe you cannot be *made* to send her to school?" demanded the pastor.

"And do *you* really believe," interrupted the old man, in a rough voice that showed his rising anger, "that on freezing mornings, when it is often stormy, I would send a little child down to the village every day? A two-hour walk — and then back again at night?"

"You are quite right, neighbor," said the pastor in a calmer voice. "So long as you live up here, it is not possible to send the child to school. But for her sake, I beg you to come down and live again in Dorfli. I cannot imagine why she has not frozen to death up here."

The Alm Uncle's eyes flashed, but he said calmly, "The child has young blood and warm clothing. And I know where to find wood and plenty of it." After a short pause, he went on in a grim voice. "As for your telling me to go back to Dorfli, Pastor — the villagers despise me and I despise them! I know you mean well, but I will *not* send the child to school, and I will *not* go back to live in Dorfli!"

"Then — may God be with you!" said the pastor sadly, and he went away.

All afternoon the Alm Uncle was silent and moody. The following morning, when Heidi asked to go down to the goatherd's cottage, he refused with a short "Not today."

Heidi said no more but busied herself about the hut. Sometime after noon, a second visitor appeared in the doorway, smartly dressed and with a jaunty feather in her hat. It was Dete.

The Alm Uncle raised his head and simply glared at her without saying a word. But Dete paid no attention and exclaimed how well Heidi was looking and how she had grown.

"But of course, Uncle," she went on, "I have always realized that she must be a burden to you. And now, Heidi," she said, "I have a wonderful surprise for you."

The Alm Uncle sat eyeing Dete in stony silence.

"The Sesemanns," Dete continued, "a very rich family in Frankfort, Germany, have a little girl who is an invalid. She has a lonely life, without any playmates, and Mr. Sesemann has instructed his housekeeper to find a nice, well-behaved child to be a companion to the little girl and to live in the house. I thought of you immediately, Heidi."

"Have you finished?" interrupted the Alm Uncle.

"Why, there isn't a soul in the world," cried Dete, "who wouldn't thank Heaven for such a splendid piece of luck!"

"Then," said the Alm Uncle, "take it to those who can better appreciate it. I will have nothing to do with it. Do you hear?"

At this, Dete lost her temper completely.

"Then you shall hear a thing or two that you won't like, Uncle!" she burst out furiously. "Don't I know that Heidi is eight years old already, and yet you refuse to send her either to school or to church? They tell me you refuse to let her learn anything! Well, she's the child of my only sister — don't forget that! If I choose to bring in the law, there isn't a soul in Dörfli who would be on your side. And if you force me to go to the law, some old matters that you'd rather keep buried may be brought to light!"

"Silence!" thundered the Alm Uncle, bringing his powerful fist down upon the table with a crash. "Take the child! Ruin her! And never bring her to me with a miserable feather in her hat and such words in her mouth as you have spoken today!"

"You have made him angry!" cried Heidi, turning upon her aunt with fire in her eyes.

"He'll get over it," said Dete shortly. "Get your things and come along."

"I won't!"

"What did you say?" Dete was furious. Then she quickly changed her tone. "Come now, Heidi," she coaxed. "It's all for your own good." As she spoke, she began to wrap up Heidi's clothes. "There, now — here's your little hat. It's shabby, but it will do."

"I'm not coming!" said Heidi.

"Don't be stubborn, Heidi. You have no idea how lovely it is in Frankfort. If you don't like it, you can come back here again — that is, if the old man gets over being angry."

"Can I come back tonight?" demanded Heidi.

"Oh, come along and don't be silly. Didn't I tell you that you can come back when you want to?" Thus did Dete succeed in coaxing Heidi down the mountain. But as they passed the goatherd's cottage, Heidi stopped.

"I can't go without saying good-by to Granny," she exclaimed.

But Dete did not let go of Heidi's hand. "You can't go to her now, Heidi. You can see her when you get back from Frankfort — and then you can bring her some nice present."

This suggestion acted like magic.

"What shall I bring her?" Heidi asked.

"Something very, very nice. For instance, they have the most delicious soft white rolls in Frankfort. She'd like them, I think."

Heidi was delighted. "That's true!" she cried. "She always gives her black bread to Peter and says it's too hard for her to eat. Oh, let's hurry, Aunt Dete! Perhaps we can get back from Frankfort tonight with the rolls!"

From that day on, when the Alm Uncle appeared in Dorfli, the villagers noticed that his face was more fierce and sullen than ever. And his dark eyes gleamed so threateningly that the mothers warned their children to keep well out of his way.

A New Life

IN THE library of the Sesemanns' large house in Frankfort, the little invalid, Clara, was lying in her wheel chair. Her blue eyes were fixed on the grandfather's clock. The hours seemed so long, and today the little girl, usually so patient, was almost fretful.

"Isn't it time *yet*, Miss Rottenmeier?" she asked at last.

The lady whom she addressed was an impressive-looking person, with an air of stiff dignity. Since the death of Clara's mother, some years before, Miss Rottenmeier had been in charge of the Sesemann household. Mr. Sesemann, who was rarely at home, had given her full authority over his domestic affairs — with the one condition that his little daughter's wishes were always to be granted.

Perhaps Miss Rottenmeier had not heard Clara's question. As she was repeating it a second time, Dete arrived at the front door with Heidi.

Dete rang the bell, and the door was opened after a time by the maid, Tinette, who seemed to be in a very bad humor.

"Well," Tinette demanded, "what is it?"

"I would like to see Miss Rottenmeier," said Dete.

Tinette turned without a word and left Dete and Heidi standing outside the door. However, she returned soon and motioned them to follow her upstairs.

In the doorway of the library Dete stopped. Miss Rottenmeier rose and came toward them, looking sharply at Heidi.

"What is your name?" the lady inquired.

"Heidi."

"Heidi? What kind of a name is that? Surely that isn't your Christian name?"

"I don't know what else it can be," said Heidi simply.

"That is not a proper answer," Miss Rottenmeier said severely. Turning to Dete, she demanded, "Is the child being impertinent?"

"With your permission, I will speak for the child," Dete said hastily, giving Heidi a little push. "It is not that she is impertinent, but that she did not understand. It is the first time she has been in such a fine house, and her manners are not what they should be — but she is a good child and obedient. Her name is Adelheid."

"Well, that is a name one can understand," said Miss Rottenmeier with great dignity. "But it seems to me that she is rather small for her age. You understand, of course, that Miss Clara's companion was to be a child her own age so that she could take part in her studies. Miss Clara is twelve years old. What is the age of this child?"

"I cannot say for certain," Dete replied smoothly. "She is a bit younger than I thought, but I believe she is about ten years old."

"I am eight years old, Aunt Dete," Heidi said clearly. "Grandfather told me so."

"What!" cried Miss Rottenmeier. "Why, that is four years too young! What were you thinking of, my good woman? Well — tell me, what books have you studied, Adelheid?"

"None," said Heidi.

"None!" Miss Rottenmeier was shocked. "Do you mean to say you don't know how to read?"

"No, I can't read, and neither can Peter."

"Merciful heavens! You can't read? What *have* you learned?"

"Nothing," Heidi replied truthfully.

There was a pause. Then Miss Rottenmeier turned a freezing gaze upon Dete. "Young woman," she said, "this was not our understanding. How dared you do this?"

Dete, however, was not easily frightened.

"I thought this child would suit you," she said smoothly. "She may be younger than expected, but older children are often disobedient. Now I must hurry away, for my lady is waiting. If you will permit, I will come again and see how the child is getting along."

So saying, she turned and went quickly from the room. After a moment, the outraged housekeeper hurried after her.

Up to this time, Clara had said nothing, but from her wheel chair had silently regarded Heidi. As soon as Miss Rottenmeier left the room, however, she beckoned to Heidi to come to her.

"Which do you like best to be called" she asked, "Heidi or Adelheid?"

"My name is Heidi and nothing else," was the reply.

"Then that is what I shall call you," said the little invalid. "I like it very much. Was your hair always short and curly like that?"

"Yes, I think so," said Heidi.

"Are you glad to have come to Frankfort?"

"No, but I am going home tomorrow, and I shall bring Granny some lovely little white rolls."

"You are a queer child," said Clara, much as a grownup would. "Don't you know that you have been brought here to live with me?

We shall have our lessons together. I'm glad you can't read, because it will be something new. You see, my tutor, Mr. Candidate, comes every morning at ten o'clock, and sometimes I think the morning will never end. But now it won't be nearly so dull."

Heidi shook her head doubtfully.

"But Heidi, you *must* learn to read," said Clara seriously.

At this moment, Miss Rottenmeier came back in a very bad temper because she had failed to catch Dete. She went into the dining room and ordered Sebastian to serve supper immediately.

The dull, formal meal began, but Heidi had already made an exciting discovery. On the snowy napkin beside her plate was a lovely soft white roll! She said nothing until Sebastian bent down to offer her some fish. Then she pointed to the roll and asked in a low voice, "Can I have that?"

Sebastian, hiding a broad grin, threw a quick side glance at Miss Rottenmeier, then nodded. Instantly, Heidi seized the roll and tucked it away in her pocket. The butler gulped— then, blank and immovable as before, he continued to offer Heidi the fish. The little girl looked up at him questioningly.

"Do I have to eat that?" she inquired. Sebastian nodded.

"Then give it to me," she said quietly.

Sebastian gulped again, and the platter began to tremble.

"You may leave the dish on the table," ordered Miss Rottenmeier, glaring at him. "I will call when I want you."

The butler hastily left the room, and Miss Rottenmeier turned to Heidi with a stern face.

"I see that there are certain things, Adelheid," she said, "which you must be made to understand immediately."

Then she began to explain all the household rules and regulations.

"You are to speak to Sebastian only when it is absolutely necessary," she said. "When you speak to me, you are always to say 'Miss Rottenmeier!'"

"She is to call me just Clara, of course," put in the little invalid.

Miss Rottenmeier drew a fresh breath and then began upon the second chapter of the household rules. There were rules for everything, it seemed — for going to bed, for getting up, for going out and for coming in, for opening doors and shutting windows.

But for Heidi, the sound of Miss Rottenmeier's voice had long since faded. Her eyes had dropped; her curly head nodded. And at last, leaning against the back of her tall, stiff chair, she slept peacefully.

"And now, Adelheid," Miss Rottenmeier wound up, "I trust you have understood me and will remember all that I have said."

There was no reply.

"She has been sound asleep for ever so long," remarked Clara. Her eyes were twinkling. Not for many a day had there been so entertaining a meal in the Sesemann household.

Miss Rottenmeier's cheeks flushed to a dull pink. "She is — outrageous!" she exclaimed. "What can one do with such a child!" But Heidi, worn out by her long journey, still slept peacefully and had to be carried up to bed.

Miss Rottenmeier Has a Hard Day

HEIDI WOKE early the next morning. Puzzled, she lay trying to think how she came to be in this huge white bed.

Heavy curtains were drawn across the window. There was a deep sofa, a dressing table, and several vases filled with flowers. And all at once, Heidi remembered that she was in Frankfort.

She sprang from the bed and ran to the window. She must see the blue sky and feel the fresh spring air against her face. But the thick curtains drawn across the windows shut these things away.

Her little arms were not strong enough to lift the heavy sash, but she pushed back the long hangings, climbed up on a chair, and peered out. Wherever she looked, she saw only walls and windows. A dreadful feeling came over her. Would she never see the green grass and breathe the sweet, clean air again? Just at that moment, there came a brisk knock at the door.

"Breakfast is ready," announced Tinette sourly.

Heidi dressed quickly and followed her to the dining room where Clara greeted her with a friendly smile.

When breakfast was over, Miss Rottenmeier told Heidi to go with Clara to the library and wait there for the tutor.

When the two children were alone, Heidi gradually began to talk about her beloved mountains and about Grandfather and Peter and Granny and the goats.

Meanwhile, Mr. Candidate arrived. Miss Rottenmeier had stayed in the dining room, but it was not long before she heard a violent crash, followed by shouts for Sebastian. She rushed to the library, then stood horrified. The table was overturned in the middle of the floor. From the midst of the scattered books a stream of ink trickled slowly across the room. Heidi was nowhere to be seen.

"Heavens above! What has happened?" cried Miss Rottenmeier. "Everything covered with ink! Ah — I know — it's that dreadful child again!"

The tutor was gazing speechlessly at the ruins, but Clara, who

was secretly enjoying herself, said, "Yes, it was Heidi, but she didn't mean to, and she must not be punished, Miss Rottenmeier. She heard some wagons go by, and she was in such a hurry to see what was happening in the street that she caught the tablecloth and pulled everything off. I don't know what can have excited her so much."

Miss Rottenmeier rushed from the room in search of Heidi. She was standing in the lower hall at the open door, looking up and down the street.

"What are you doing? How dare you run away from your lessons like this?" demanded Miss Rottenmeier.

"I heard pine trees rustling," said Heidi. "But I can't hear them now."

"Pine trees! What are you talking about? Come upstairs at once and see the mischief you have done!"

Heidi followed the angry housekeeper up the stairs.

"Never," said Miss Rottenmeier, pointing to the library floor, "*never* let this happen again."

Lessons were out of the question for the rest of the day.

In the early afternoon, Clara always had to rest for two hours. Heidi had been told that she was free to amuse herself. So, when luncheon was over, she approached Sebastian and said she had something to ask him.

"Well, well," said Sebastian, "what do you want me to do?"

"How can a person get a window open, Sebastian?" she asked.

"Why, just like this," he said, and flung open the dining room window. Then he drew up a wooden bench for her to stand on. "Want to see what is going on below you?"

But after a moment or two, poor Heidi climbed down. "There's nothing but a stony street down there," she said woefully. "Where can I go to see all over?"

"You'd have to get high up, in a tower, I guess," said Sebastian, "like that golden steeple over there."

Instantly, Heidi darted from the room, down the stairs, and into the street. She spied a young organ grinder standing on the curb. His hand organ was on his back.

Heidi ran up to him and asked, "Do you know where the church with the golden steeple is?"

"Sure I do."

"Then will you please show me where it is?"

"First, show *me* what you'll give me," said the boy.

"What do you want?" asked Heidi.

"Money."

"I haven't got any, but Clara has, and she will give me some. How much do you want?"

"Twenty cents."

"All right. Come on."

They reached the steps of an old church. Heidi had already discovered the bell and now pushed it.

"You must wait for me here," she said, "because I don't know how to find the way back."

At that moment the doors were unbolted, and a little old man stood there, dressed in a long black gown.

"I want to go up in the steeple and look at the view," said Heidi.

"Be off with you!" was the indignant reply.

Just before the door shut, Heidi cried imploringly, "Oh, please — *please!* Just this once!" Her black eyes were so earnest that the old man melted in spite of himself.

Clinging to the sexton's hand, Heidi began to climb the narrow, winding staircase of the tower. Up, up, they went until at last they reached the very top.

"Well, here we are," said her companion.

He lifted her in his arms so she could look out of the little window. For several minutes Heidi gazed down upon the roofs and chimneys.

"It isn't what I thought I'd see," she said hopelessly.

"Well, that's the only thing there is to see," said the sexton.

He led the way down the dark stairway, with Heidi following, until the steps widened at a landing. Here stood a basket, in front of which a large gray cat lay purring loudly.

"Come over here," said the old man. "The little ones are in the basket."

Heidi rushed to his side. Then she clapped her hands in delight, for in the basket eight furry little kittens sprawled, clawing and scratching each other with their tiny, feeble paws.

"Oh, the dear, *dear* little things!" shrieked Heidi rapturously.

"Would you like to take one or two of them home with you?" asked the sexton, smiling.

Heidi was dumb with joy. She chose two of the kittens, a white one and a tawny one, and stowed them away in the pockets of her pinafore. Then the sexton led her down the tower stairs to the church door, where the young organ grinder was waiting for her.

"Now," said Heidi, "which way is the Sesemanns' house?"

"Come on," he said, and set off at a run. Heidi and her pocketful of kittens scampered along beside him. In a very few minutes he had brought her to the house.

"So, *there* you are!" exclaimed Sebastian, as he opened the door for her. "In with you, quick, ma'amselle — Miss Rottenmeier looks like a loaded cannon! What ever made you go running off?"

Heidi entered the dining room and took her place at the table in the midst of a dead silence. Clara did not speak. Miss Rottenmeier did not so much as raise her eyes. The meal proceeded for several minutes without a word being uttered. Then Miss Rottenmeier pursed her lips, assumed a stern expression, and began:

"Adelheid, I shall have more to say to you later on. But for the present, I wish you to distinctly *understand* that you have been a *very* bad girl. To run away from the house — without permission — without a word to anyone — and to return at *this hour* — is a piece of naughtiness that deserves *severe* punishment!"

Meow! was the reply to this outburst.

Miss Rottenmeier's sallow face flushed red with anger. "What do you mean by such impudence, Adelheid!" she cried. "What —"

"But I —" Heidi began.

Meow! Meow!

"That is *enough!*" said Miss Rottenmeier, almost choking. "Leave the room *instantly!*"

Heidi stood up obediently, but she was frightened and still trying to offer an explanation.

"Indeed, Miss Rottenmeier, I meant —"

Meow! Meow! Meow!

"But Heidi," cried Clara in distress, "when you see how angry you have made Miss Rottenmeier, why do you keep on saying, 'Meow'?"

"But it's not me — it's the kittens," said Heidi, and with that she brought forth her two treasures.

If she had flung a bomb on the table, she could not have produced a more startling effect.

"What! KITTENS!!" shrieked Miss Rottenmeier, leaping up from her chair. "Sebastian! Tinette! Take these horrible animals away!"

To the poor woman there was nothing on earth more terrifying than a cat. She rushed into the library, bolting the door behind her.

Sebastian was choking with laughter behind the dining room door. At last he tried to obey the commands of the panic-stricken housekeeper. But in the dining room he found Clara cuddling one of the kittens in her lap, while Heidi played with the other one.

Sebastian readily promised to make a bed for them and to put them "where the lady won't lay eyes on 'em."

At this point, the library door was timidly opened a crack, and Miss Rottenmeier called, "Have those dreadful animals been taken away?"

"Yes, ma'am," said Sebastian respectfully, and with that he quickly picked up the kittens and disappeared.

Miss Rottenmeier was too exhausted by what she had been through to do more than order both children to bed immediately. But although the remainder of Heidi's scolding was yet to come, the kittens were safely established in the Sesemann household.

New Disturbances

SEBASTIAN HAD just ushered Mr. Candidate into the library the next morning when the doorbell rang again loudly. The butler opened the door to find a ragged lad with a hand organ strapped to his back standing there.

"What do you want?" Sebastian asked haughtily.

"I want to see Clara," was the answer.

"And what might you be wanting of *Miss* Clara, pray?"

"She owes me forty cents," said the boy coolly.

"Indeed? And how do you know a Miss Clara lives here?"

"Yesterday I took her where she wanted to go, and that was twenty cents, and then I brought her here, and that was another twenty cents."

"Well, that just shows what a rogue you are," Sebastian cried, "because Miss Clara can't walk! So take yourself off instantly."

But the boy did not move. "I tell you, I saw her on the street yesterday," he insisted. "She has short black hair and black eyes."

"Oho!" Sebastian began to chuckle. "That was little ma'amselle
— up to something new. Well, step inside and wait here in the hall."

Then, in quite a good humor, he went up to the library.

"There's a lad downstairs who wishes to speak to Miss Clara," he
announced. Clara, only too glad of an interruption, asked the tutor's
permission to have the boy brought up at once.

As usual, during the lesson hour, Miss Rottenmeier was sitting
in the dining room, her bony fingers busy with her needlework. Suddenly she sat up with a jerk.

From somewhere there drifted to her ears the merry tones of a
hand organ. They sounded curiously near at hand — indeed, one
might even suppose that they came from the library!

Miss Rottenmeier rose abruptly and, going to the door of the
other room, flung it open. For a moment she could not believe her
eyes. It was *unthinkable!* Clara and Heidi were listening with beaming
faces while a little ragamuffin was standing in the middle of the room,
grinding away at a hand organ with all his might.

"Stop!" screamed Miss Rottenmeier. "Stop immediately! This
instant!" But her words were drowned by the cheery music.

She made a rush toward the boy — then something moved directly
between her feet. She glanced down. And there, stirring clumsily on
the floor, she beheld a large, sluggish turtle! With a wild leap,
Miss Rottenmeier swept her skirts around her and shrieked at the top
of her lungs for Sebastian.

"Take these — Put them out! Send them away!" gasped poor
Miss Rottenmeier, collapsing into the nearest chair.

Secretly delighted, Sebastian told the boy to take his turtle and
organ and go. But before he let the youngster out into the street, he
slipped some coins into his dirty little hand.

"Forty for yesterday, and forty for playing," Sebastian said with a grin. "Well done!"

In the next few days, Miss Rottenmeier's resentment against Heidi increased rather than lessened. It seemed to her that since the child's coming, the whole household had been thrown out of gear. But Clara was never bored now, for even during their lessons, Heidi was amusing. And when the lessons were over, she would sit beside Clara and talk about life on the Alm.

But finally her yearning for her grandfather and her old life became unbearable. She remembered that Dete had promised she could go home whenever she wanted. Now, at last, Heidi felt that she could not stand this separation from all the things she loved.

The next afternoon she packed her long-hoarded rolls in the old red shawl, put on her battered straw hat, and hurried quietly downstairs. But just as she reached the entrance, Miss Rottenmeier appeared.

For a moment the astonished housekeeper merely stood still and looked at Heidi. Then she burst out, "What does this mean? I forbade you to leave this house without permission and go roaming around."

"But I wasn't going to roam around," answered Heidi, frightened. "I am only going home. I must go home," she sobbed. "Granny is waiting for me, and Snowhopper will be crying because I am not there, and if I don't give Peter my bread and cheese, he will beat Thistlefinch. Here one never sees how the sun says good night to the mountains, and the eagle never flies over Frankfort —"

"Mercy on us!" exclaimed Miss Rottenmeier. "The child is out of her mind! Go up to your room at once."

Heidi started up the stairs slowly and dejectedly. Without a word, she went into her room and closed the door.

At supper that night, Heidi, when she had put away the roll for Granny in her pocket, sat as quiet as a mouse, eating nothing, drinking nothing, saying nothing.

The next morning, since Mr. Sesemann was expected home soon, Miss Rottenmeier went up to inspect Heidi's clothes. She was anxious to have Clara's father see what good care she took of the little girl. A few moments later, she came marching down to the library holding a bundle out in front of her at arm's length.

"What is this that I have found now, Adelheid?" she cried. "In your wardrobe — a place for dresses — a *pile of stale bread!* Tinette! See that all this stale bread is thrown away immediately, and also the old straw hat on Miss Adelheid's table."

"No! No! Not my hat!" shrieked Heidi, springing up. "And the bread is for Granny, Miss Rottenmeier. You must not throw it away!"

"Stay here, Adelheid," Miss Rottenmeier said sharply.

Heidi flung herself down beside Clara's chair, weeping as if her heart would break. Miss Rottenmeier left the room.

"Heidi, listen," begged Clara. "Don't cry so! You can take all the rolls you want to Granny. The bread you had was too stale to eat anyway. So don't — *don't* cry."

"You *promise* that I can have just as many as I had saved?"

"Many, many more, Heidi. I promise."

At last Heidi dried her eyes. But her face was still red and tear-stained when she came to supper.

Meanwhile, Sebastian was trying to signal to her. He made faces, pointed to her head and then to his own, and finally winked mysteriously, as if to say, "Don't worry. I've taken care of things."

But not until Heidi was going to bed did she discover his meaning.

The kind-hearted fellow had taken the battered hat off the rubbish heap and hidden it under the bedspread in Heidi's room.

Thus it was that Heidi, creeping under the covers to cry herself to sleep, found the precious hat. In the joy of this discovery, the loss of the rolls was forgotten. She hugged the old hat in her arms. Then, scrambling out of bed, she wrapped it up carefully in a big handkerchief and thrust it into the most secret corner of her wardrobe.

MR. SESEMANN had come home at last. The whole household was in a state of excitement. He greeted Clara first, for father and daughter had a strong, tender affection for each other. Heidi had retreated shyly to a corner, but after a moment Mr. Sesemann called to her. Holding out his hand, he said kindly, "So this is the little Swiss girl. Come and shake hands with me, Heidi. Now, tell me, how are you two girls getting along together? No quarreling?"

"Oh, no. Clara is always good to me," said Heidi.

"And Heidi never quarrels," said Clara.

"Well, that's good to hear." Mr. Sesemann stood up, looking pleased. "Now, you must let me go to get a bite to eat. And afterwards, you shall see what I've brought you." And he went to the dining room where Sebastian had set out some luncheon for him. Here Miss Rottenmeier was waiting, eager for a chance to speak to him.

"Mr. Sesemann," she announced, "we have been deceived!"

"How, may I ask?" inquired Mr. Sesemann calmly.

"I am sure that this child is not in her right mind!"

"Not in her right mind!" By this time, Mr. Sesemann was utterly bewildered. "I must go and speak to my daughter," he said, cutting the conversation short, and hastened out of the dining room.

He found the two children still in the library. Seating himself by Clara's side, he quietly asked Heidi, "My dear, will you run and bring me a glass of water?"

And Heidi darted away to do his bidding.

"Now, Clara darling," said Mr. Sesemann, taking his daughter's hand in his, "can you tell me what earthly reason Miss Rottenmeier can possibly have for thinking Heidi is not in her right mind?"

Clara *could* tell him, and when he had heard about the kittens that had frightened Miss Rottenmeier so badly and the little organ grinder and his turtles, he threw back his head and laughed.

"Well — do you want me to send her away, my dear?" he asked.

"Oh, no, Papa!" cried Clara. "Don't send Heidi away. Ever since she has been here, everything has been so much more fun."

That evening Mr. Sesemann told Miss Rottenmeier that Heidi would not be sent away.

Mr. Sesemann had to make another business trip to Paris. But he promised Clara that her grandmother would soon be with her. He had, in fact, hardly gone when preparations began for the arrival of old Mrs. Sesemann.

Late one evening the sound of carriage wheels brought Sebastian and Tinette hurrying to the front door. Miss Rottenmeier followed.

Heidi had been told that she must not go downstairs until she was sent for. Obediently, the child sat patiently in a corner of her bedroom. After some time, Tinette's head appeared around the door.

"You are to go to the library," snapped the maid.

Heidi trotted down the stairs. As she opened the door of the library, a fresh, friendly voice called to her.

"Ah, here is the child! Come here and let me look at you."

Heidi walked over to Mrs. Sesemann's chair.

"You must call me Grandmamma, as Clara does," said the old lady gaily. "Can you remember to do that?"

"Oh, yes," said Heidi, and added honestly, "because that is what I have always called you."

"Did you, indeed? Well, that's all right," and Grandmamma laughed again, so kindly and merrily that Heidi loved her at once.

"And now, tell me *your* name," she said, taking Heidi's hand.

"My name is Heidi — but if I am called Adelheid, I will answer."

"Mrs. Sesemann, you will agree that the child cannot be called by a ridiculous nickname," said Miss Rottenmeier.

"My dear Miss Rottenmeier, if she is accustomed to being called Heidi, I can see no reason why she should *not* be called so."

Mrs. Sesemann was a very keen old lady, indeed. She had guessed immediately how matters stood in her son's household.

The next day, after luncheon, when Clara was resting, Grandmamma went to Miss Rottenmeier's room and knocked at the door.

"Will you bring Heidi to my sitting room, please?" Mrs. Sesemann asked. "I want to show her a book I brought with me."

"But the child knows nothing whatever about books," Miss Rottenmeier sighed. "She has not been able to learn even her ABC's."

"That is odd," Mrs. Sesemann commented thoughtfully. "She doesn't look like a child who cannot learn."

When, a few minutes later, Mrs. Sesemann greeted Heidi at the sitting room door, she made her sit down in a little chair beside her own. Then she began to show her the colored pictures in the book.

Heidi looked on, enraptured. Grandmamma said, "Now, Heidi, tell me, how are the lessons going? Are you learning to read?"

"Oh, no," Heidi answered with a sigh. "It is impossible."

"Wherever did you get that idea?" Mrs. Sesemann asked.

"Peter told me, and he knows, because he has tried to learn."

"Well," said Mrs. Sesemann, "I don't know Peter, but let me tell you this, Heidi. We must not let other people's failures discourage us. When you are able to read, you shall have this book all for yourself, and you will be able to find out for yourself what happened. Now let us go and see Clara. Bring the book with you, and we'll show her the beautiful pictures."

Mrs. Sesemann's sympathy brought comfort to the homesick little girl, but it could not lift the heavy burden on her heart. She understood at last that her Aunt Dete had deceived her. She was not to be allowed to go back to her grandfather whenever she wished. On the contrary, she might have to live in Frankfort for a long, long time.

The child's melancholy did not escape Mrs. Sesemann.

It was about a week later that Grandmamma went into the library to see how Heidi was coming along.

The two children were sitting side by side. Heidi was reading aloud — slowly, perhaps, but distinctly and correctly.

That same night, the little girl found the picture book lying on her plate at supper. She glanced up in surprise, and Grandmamma nodded gaily. "Yes, it's yours now, as I promised, my dear."

The wonderful book became Heidi's dearest possession. Every evening she read aloud from it to Clara and Grandmamma.

But although the little girl enjoyed her new interests, there was sadness in her black eyes. And after Grandmamma left to return to her own home, Heidi could not force herself to eat. Every day she grew paler and thinner. At night, she cried, smothering her tears in her pillow, until she had wept herself to sleep.

The Haunted House

AN EVENT both strange and weird began to happen again and again in the Sesemann house. Every morning, when the servants came downstairs, the front door would be found standing wide open. The first time it happened, they thought that burglars had broken in during the night, but nothing was ever missing.

At last, Mr. Sesemann, who had returned home from Paris for a few days, decided to sit up all night to find the solution of the mystery. Doctor Classen, an old friend — and the family physician — volunteered to keep him company.

The two men went into a room off the corridor to keep their watch. The door was left slightly ajar, so that while the light did not shine out into the corridor, it was possible to hear the least sound.

When midnight struck, the doctor remarked, "Perhaps the ghost is too clever for us and won't come tonight."

Another hour passed.

Suddenly the doctor raised a finger. "Sh! Did you hear anything then, Sesemann?" he whispered.

Both listened, holding their breath. Then each man took a candle and stepped softly out into the corridor.

The front door was wide open, and the bright moonlight streaming in showed a white form that stood on the threshold.

"Who is there?" shouted the doctor in a voice of thunder. Both men rushed at the white figure, which turned around with a low cry.

Heidi, clad only in her little white nightgown, looked up in terror at the lights and trembled from head to foot.

The two men looked at each other, astonished.

"What are you doing here, Heidi?" Mr. Sesemann asked gently.

"I don't know," said Heidi dully.

"I think this is my problem, Sesemann," said the doctor. "Wait for me in your sitting room, and I will take the child back to bed."

He led Heidi up the stairs. When they reached her room, he carried her tenderly to her bed and covered her warmly.

"Now tell me, where did you want to go?" the doctor asked.

"I didn't want to go anywhere," Heidi said, still trembling a little. "I didn't go downstairs myself — I was just there all of a sudden."

"Did you have a dream?"

"Oh, yes, I dream the same thing every night — always that I am with Grandfather again — and I hear the wind blowing through the fir trees, and I run to the door of the hut and open it. Then I wake up — and I am still in Frankfort."

"Hmm. And do you feel any pain — in your head or your back?"

"No — just here in my chest — as if I wanted to cry."

"I see. Do you like being in Frankfort?"

Heidi could not answer.

"Hmm. And where was it you lived with your grandfather?"

"Up on the Alm —"

"And you never found it lonely there?"

"Oh, no, it was *beautiful!*" And Heidi burst into sobs.

The doctor rose. "There, now — cry, Heidi, for it will do you good," he said, laying her head gently back on the pillows. "Then try to sleep. Tomorrow everything is going to be all right."

He left the room and rejoined Mr. Sesemann.

"My friend," the doctor said soberly, "your ghost is Heidi, who has been sleepwalking every night. She is wasting away from homesickness. There is no time to be lost. She *must* be sent home immediately!"

Mr. Sesemann was shocked. "Sleepwalking — ill — wasting away from homesickness! All this in my house and no one noticed it? But you cannot ask me to send her back to her people ill when she came to us sound and healthy!"

"Sesemann, I tell you the child must go home — tomorrow!"

It was daylight when the doctor finally departed, and Mr. Sesemann finally knew he must send Heidi back to her mountain home.

GREATLY DISTURBED, Mr. Sesemann went upstairs and called together all the servants. Johann was sent to order the horses and carriage. Tinette was to dress Heidi for traveling as soon as the child wakened. Miss Rottenmeier was to see that Heidi's things were packed at once. Then Mr. Sesemann hurried away to his daughter's room.

Clara begged her father to find some way of curing Heidi without sending her away, but Mr. Sesemann felt he must do as the doctor ordered. He promised Clara that he would take her to Switzerland to visit Heidi the following year. After that, Clara said no more.

Mr. Sesemann sent for Heidi and said gaily, "Well, little Heidi, what have you to say now? You are going home — right away!"

"Home!" echoed Heidi. Her face turned pale with joy.

"Yes. And now you must eat a hearty breakfast, so sit down," said Mr. Sesemann. "The carriage will be at the door soon."

Heidi tried to eat, but she could not swallow a morsel. Mr. Sesemann did not urge her, but merely bade her run up and say good-by to Clara. It was just what Heidi was longing to do, and she ran off.

"Look, Heidi!" Clara called from the bed.

There were dresses, handkerchiefs, underclothes, sweaters for her — and best of all, in a pretty basket, a dozen lovely soft white rolls for Granny! Heidi jumped for joy.

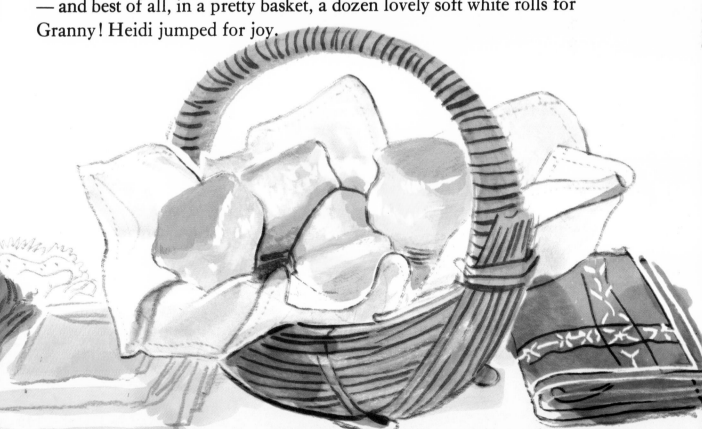

The two children had forgotten how soon Heidi was leaving, and when Mr. Sesemann called her, there was no time for tears. Heidi rushed to her room. Her precious book was still there, and her old straw hat and the red shawl. She tied these treasures carefully in the shawl. Then, putting on her pretty new hat, she left the room.

Taking Mr. Sesemann's hand, Heidi thanked him very sincerely for all his kindness to her. "And tell the doctor I thank him too," she added shyly. Then she climbed into the carriage, followed by Sebastian, who carried a large basket of provisions, and the carriage rolled away.

The next morning, after several hours of traveling, they arrived at Mayenfeld. Here Sebastian looked about the platform for someone who might direct him to Dorfli. A sturdy, broad-shouldered man was loading sacks into a small wagon. Sebastian approached him, and the man, who was going up to Dorfli, agreed to take Heidi and her trunk as far as the village in his wagon.

The clock in the belfry of the little mountain church was just striking five when the wagoner lifted the little girl down from the seat. She thanked him and told him her grandfather would come for her trunk the next day. Then Heidi ran up the mountain path.

At last she reached the goatherd's cottage. She was trembling so much that she could hardly lift the latch of the door. But in another moment she was peering into the dimness of the tiny room.

"Oh," murmured a low, sad voice in the dark corner by the chimney, "that is the way Heidi used to run in. Who is there?"

"It *is* Heidi, Granny!" And with that Heidi flung herself into the old woman's arms and clung to her. The grandmother passed a trembling hand over the child's short, curly hair.

"Oh, Heidi, Heidi, is it really you?"

"Yes, Granny, and now that I have come back, I shall never go away again. See what I have brought you!" Diving into her basket, Heidi brought out the white rolls and laid them one by one on Granny's knee, until it seemed to the old woman that there was no end to them.

"Child, child, what blessings have you brought me?" exclaimed Granny. "But the best of all blessings is yourself."

As they were talking, Brigida entered the room. Seeing the little girl, she stopped short in amazement. "Heidi!" she gasped.

Heidi stood up and gave her her hand.

"What a lovely dress you are wearing!" exclaimed Brigida. "And see the pretty hat with the feather! Let me see how it looks on you."

"No, no — I don't want it," Heidi said quickly. "If you like it, you can have it, because I don't need it. I have my own."

She untied the old shawl and took out the battered straw hat. It looked even more battered than ever, but Heidi didn't care. When her Aunt Dete had taken her away, Grandfather had called after them that he never wanted to see her wearing a fine-feathered hat like Dete's. It was because of this that Heidi had kept the shabby old hat so carefully.

"Now I must go to Grandfather," she said, taking the old woman's hand gently, "but tomorrow I will come again."

With her basket on her arm, she set out up the mountain once more. The sun was just beginning to sink behind the vast snowfields, and the whole scene was colored with its splendor.

Now at last she saw the hut before her. And there, seated on the bench — his pipe between his lips, just as when she had first seen him — was the solitary figure of the Alm Uncle.

Heidi rushed to him. Throwing her basket on the ground, she clasped her arms around him, crying over and over in breathless joy.

"Grandfather! Grandfather! Grandfather!"

He did not speak. For the first time in long, long years his eyes were wet. Then very gently he took her hand, and together they went into the hut. And that night Heidi's sleep was deep and sweet.

Sunday Morning

HEIDI STOOD under the pine trees, waiting for her grandfather to take her down to the goatherd's hut. She was to stay there while he went to Dorfli to get her trunk. Soon he appeared, and hand in hand they started down the path.

When they reached the cottage, Heidi ran eagerly in to Granny and asked how the rolls tasted. Granny declared they were delicious.

At that moment Heidi's eye fell on a worn old hymnbook lying on a shelf.

"Granny, do you know that I can read now?" she cried. "Would you like me to read you a hymn from your hymnbook?"

"Read!" exclaimed Granny in amazement. "Is it possible? Oh, if I could hear one of the old hymns, I would be so happy!"

So Heidi climbed upon a chair and got down the old book. She asked which hymn she should read.

"Whichever one you like, child," said Granny. She stopped her spinning wheel and waited breathlessly for Heidi to begin.

"Here is one about the sun, Granny," said Heidi. "I'll read this."

As she read on, Granny sat perfectly still, tears of joy running down her cheeks. When Heidi finished, she exclaimed, "Oh, Heidi, it seems as if the light had really come again. It shines in my heart."

A little later, the Alm Uncle tapped at the window and signaled to Heidi that it was time to go home.

Early the next morning, the Alm Uncle was standing at the door of the hut. It was Sunday, and already the church bells were ringing.

"Come, Heidi, the sun is up," he called. "Put on your best dress. We must go to church together."

Heidi hurried to join her grandfather. When she saw him she stopped short in delight. "Grandfather, how nice you look!" she cried, clapping her hands. "I never saw you in your Sunday coat before, and I *never* saw you look so lovely."

The old man smiled. "You look very fine yourself," he said. "Now let us go."

Nearly all the good folk of Dorfli were already in church when Heidi and the Alm Uncle entered and slipped into a pew near the door. But in the middle of the first hymn, one of the congregation, who was sitting nearby, nudged his neighbor and whispered in amazement, "Look! The Alm Uncle is in church!"

The other looked, gaped, and nudged his neighbor. In less than a minute the whisper had spread through the whole church. "The Alm Uncle is here. See, the Alm Uncle is here!"

At the end of the service, the Alm Uncle took Heidi's hand and walked with her from the church to the parish house. The pastor himself opened the door. He shook the old man's hand warmly.

"I have come, Pastor," said the Alm Uncle slowly, "to ask your pardon for what I said to you that day on the Alm. In all that you said you were right, and I was wrong. This winter we are going to come down to Dorfli to live during the cold weather. And if the village people shun me when I come back among them, it will be no more than I deserve — but I think that *you* will not turn away from me."

The pastor's eyes shone with pleasure, and he took the old man's hand once more and pressed it warmly.

"My friend," he said, "you will never regret the day you decided to come back and live among us. As for myself, I am looking forward to passing many a long winter's evening with you at the fireside. And the child will certainly find good friends among us."